Pearl's Passover

A Family Celebration through Stories, Recipes, Crafts, and Songs

WRITTEN AND ILLUSTRATED BY
JANE BRESKIN ZALBEN

SIMON & SCHUSTER BOOKS FOR YOUNG READERS

New York   London   Toronto   Sydney   Singapore

ALSO ABOUT PEARL AND HER FAMILY:

Pearl Plants a Tree

Pearl's Marigolds for Grandpa

Pearl's Eight Days of Chanukah

More books by Jane Breskin Zalben:

Unfinished Dreams

To Every Season

The Magic Menorah

Appreciation goes to Anahid Hamparian and Paul Zakris, once again for their efforts, and to Jessica Schulte, who put so much editorial care into every single word, I thank you. Last, to Steven Zalben for the "journey" literally on the page and off.

SIMON & SCHUSTER BOOKS FOR YOUNG READERS
An imprint of Simon & Schuster Children's Publishing Division
1230 Avenue of the Americas, New York, New York 10020
PEARL'S PASSOVER: A FAMILY CELEBRATION THROUGH STORIES, RECIPES, CRAFTS, AND SONGS
copyright © 2002 Jane Breskin Zalben
The papyrus used on the jacket and title page of this book was brought back by the author from the Nile River in Egypt.
The map of the exodus on page 21 was drawn by Steven Zalben.
The music on pages 43, 45, and 47 was arranged by Jonathan Zalben.
All rights reserved, including the right of reproduction in whole or in part in any form.
SIMON & SCHUSTER BOOKS FOR YOUNG READERS *is a trademark of Simon & Schuster.*

Printed in Hong Kong

2 4 6 8 10 9 7 5 3 1

Library of Congress Cataloging-in-Publication Data
Zalben, Jane Breskin.
Pearl's passover: a family celebration through stories, recipes, crafts, and songs / written and illustrated by
Jane Breskin Zalben.   p.   cm.
Summary: As an extended family prepares for their Passover celebration, they explain
the various customs and traditions related to this holiday. Includes various related activities.
ISBN 0-689-81487-9
[1. Passover—Fiction. 2. Seder—Fiction. 3. Jews—United States—Fiction. 4. Handicraft.]
I. Title.
PZ7.Z254 Pdm 2002
[Fic]—dc21   2001020580

Book design by Jane Breskin Zalben
The text for this book is set in Bembo.
The illustrations are rendered in gold leaf, colored pencils, and watercolor
with a triple-zero sable brush on Opaline Parchment.

Contents

SPRING CLEANING

Pearl was painting a welcome scroll for the front door.
"They're coming ba-a-ck," she cried out.
"Who?" asked her brother, Avi.
"The two terrors of Teaneck. *The twins.*"
"Cousins Sophie and Harry?" Avi asked his big sister.
"Yup," said Pearl. "They're staying over during Passover."
"Both seders?" Avi trembled. "And all eight days?"
"I think so," Pearl answered. "Remember last Chanukah,
when Harry made a menorah out of Sophie's hair curlers?"
Avi added, "And Sophie tried to slip a *latke* on your chair."
"How could I forget," Pearl groaned.
Mama smiled to herself as she overheard Pearl and Avi.
"The whole family is coming to cook and get the house ready,"
she said, emptying the cabinets of pasta, rice, and grains
while Papa lined the kitchen shelves with shiny new paper.
"Spring cleaning." Papa winked. Mama smiled back at him.
"We wouldn't want any bread crumbs left," Papa said.
"I'm spring cleaning, too," Avi said, giggling as he bit a cookie.
"So am I," said Pearl, munching from a box of granola.
Papa snapped a pretzel in half. "I'll help," he teased.
Mama made an enormous pot of pasta—enough to feed an army.
They ate so much trying to get rid of the *chametz*, no one
could move an inch. Mama chuckled, "It's not even the
first Seder yet and already everyone's stuffed and sleepy."

*Leaping
on the
mountains
the time of
singing has come*

PASSOVER SCROLL FOR FRONT DOOR OR
WELCOME WALL HANGING

Pearl and Avi and their parents wanted to hang something on the front door to welcome guests. Their scroll has pictures and words. Papa remembered a poem written by a Jew in Germany in 1939. It reminded him of another hard time in the history of the Jewish people: "I believe in the sun even when it is not shining. I believe in love even when I do not feel. I believe in God even when God is silent." Mama chose a line from the Song of Songs: "Leaping on the mountains . . . the time of singing has come." Mama said, "It gives the feeling of the Seder and springtime." Pearl wrote, "Next Year in Jerusalem!"—which is said at the end of the Seder. Pearl read to Avi to give him many ideas. He finally decided to write the Hebrew word for "welcome, hello, and peace," Shalom.

2 tree branches	Poster paint
Brown paper or shopping bag	Twine or rope
Ruler, scissors, hole puncher	White glue
Sand, dried grass, or straw for border decoration	

1. Find two thin straight branches as thick as pencils about 13-15 inches long.
2. Cut a 12″ x 16″ rectangle from brown paper. You can use a shopping bag. This will be the banner of the wall hanging.
3. With a hole puncher, make six holes 2 inches apart from each other at the top and bottom of the banner.
4. Using poster paint, decorate the scroll. Don't forget to leave room for the quotation, or your own saying.
5. Loop twine or rope around stick and then once or twice through holes to attach scroll to twigs. Knot twine at either end. The aim is to fasten twigs to the paper. (See diagram.)
6. Border design (optional): Make a line ½ inch from the edge of banner with white glue. Dust with sand. (Or, instead of sand, glue dried grass or straw to look like reeds. Or, discover materials in your own yard, park, or beach to use!) When glue is thoroughly dry, carefully lift scroll over newspaper (or take it outside) to remove loose sand or grass.

THE FAMILY ARRIVES

Pearl and Avi played outside waiting for the family to arrive.
Flowers and trees were blooming everywhere. Avi lay on his stomach
picking clover while Mama mixed a batch of *mandelbrot* inside the house.
She stared out the screen door every few minutes. "Are they here yet?"
While they waited, she gave Pearl and Avi a peek at the batter.
"Too many cranberries?" Mama asked.
Avi nodded yes, making a sour face.
"More cinnamon, Mama," said Pearl.
"With experts like these, who could go wrong?" Mama grinned as she wiped
her hands on the dish towel and carried the mixing bowl back inside.
When Pearl saw Papa's yellow car turning the corner,
she shouted, "Grandma and Grandpa are here!"
Mama ran to the front door with open arms.
There were so many bundles, shopping bags, suitcases, and packages,
Mama could barely hug her parents. Pearl and Avi got mushy wet kisses.
"A little something." Grandma handed them each a box of macaroons.
Grandpa said, "Enough *shmoozing*, we have a lot of work to do!"
Everybody began cooking up a storm. Grandma made her famous brisket.
Grandpa smelled up the house with his homemade *gefilte fish*.
Mama and Papa were the official tasters. "Less salt! What is this, the Dead Sea?"
With laughter in the air, Uncle Solly came in the back door to the kitchen
carrying a huge bowl of *matzoh balls*, each one the size of baseball.
"You shouldn't have," Mama said, sighing.
"What's family for?" insisted Aunt Rachel, following him,
as she handed Mama two kinds of *ḥaroset*. Mama smiled gratefully.
Pearl noticed Cousin Sophie. "I like your new pink shoes."

"Oh, these?" Sophie made sure the light hit them so they glowed.

"Bet I find the *afikomen* this year," Cousin Harry said to Avi with a smirk.

Pearl and Avi noticed Harry's brand-new running sneakers for racing.

Avi found the hidden matzoh last year, and Harry was not a happy camper.

"They're ba-a-a-ck," Pearl muttered to Avi, who just shook his head.

MAMA'S CRANBERRY MANDELBROT

Mama is getting a little wild and crazy (or, as her mother put it, "a bissel meshuga"). One year, she threw morsels of white chocolate into the mandelbrot. Another year, she experimented with shavings of bittersweet chocolate and a pinch of instant coffee to give these cookies a mocha flavor. This year, the crimson cranberries looked so good in the supermarket, Mama said, "Hey, why not try these this year?" Mandelbrot is Yiddish for "almond bread."

4 extra large eggs	1/4 teaspoon salt (optional)
1 1/2 cups granulated sugar	2–3 cups Passover cake meal
1 teaspoon vanilla extract	1/4 teaspoon potato starch
1/2 teaspoon almond extract (optional)	1/4 teaspoon grated lemon rind (lemon zest)
Pinch of ground cinnamon	1 cup whole or slivered almonds, chopped
1/2 cup vegetable oil	1 cup dried cranberries

1. Preheat oven to 350 degrees Farenheit.
2. In a large bowl, beat together eggs, sugar, vanilla and almond extracts, and cinnamon. Add oil and blend.
3. In a separate mixing bowl, sift together salt, Passover cake meal, and potato starch.
4. Add lemon rind to dry ingredients. Then blend wet ingredients into dry mixture.
5. Chop almonds in blender or food processor. Add dried cranberries and fold into dough.
6. Pour batter 1 inch deep (scooping with a spatula) into three separate 4 1/2″ x 9″ greased baking pans. Bake about 30 minutes. Remove from pans. Cut into 1/2″ to 1″ slices. (Grandma likes thin slices. Grandpa likes them thick. "To each his own," they both say.)
7. Place slices onto cookie sheet and toast in oven at 375 degrees for another 10 minutes.

Yield: 3 loaves or about 4-5 dozen sliced "cookies"
Note: Mandelbrot will stay fresh all eight days of Passover.
Serve with "a glass tea" or a cup of tea! And dunk!

APPLE-AND-WALNUT HAROSET

Aunt Rachel's mother is Ashkenazi and comes from Poland. Eastern European Jews use this recipe. Haroset represents the mortar used by the Israelites as they labored for the Pharoahs.

3-4 cups shelled walnuts, minced

5-6 cups sweet apples, peeled and chopped

Rind of 1 lemon, finely grated (lemon zest)

1-2 tablespoons maple syrup or 1/4 cup granulated sugar.

1 teaspoon ground cinnamon

1/4 teaspoon ground nutmeg

1/2 cup Concord grape wine

Matzoh (to make sandwich of haroset and bitter herbs—*korekh*)

1. Mix all ingredients together in a food processor or blender; or for a chunkier consistency, grind by hand with a mortar and pestle. Chill until ready to use for the Seder.
2. Spread a full teaspoon of haroset "paste" on about a 2″ x 3″ piece of broken matzoh.
   Yield: Serves about 25 (with plenty left over for second helpings!).

AUNT RACHEL'S DATE-AND-ALMOND HAROSET

Aunt Rachel is a Sephardic Jew. Her family is from Morocco. The Sephardim are Jews who come from the Middle East, the Mediterranean, India, and North African countries. There are many different kinds of haroset depending on what part of the world Jews come from. Some Sephardic Jews add cloves, cardamom, ginger, dried apricots, or candied orange peel to create "the fruit-and-nuts mortar" for the haroset.

3 cups dates, pitted

1 cup blanched, shelled almonds, minced

Rind of 1 lemon, finely grated (lemon zest)

1/2 teaspoon orange peel, finely grated

1/2 teaspoon ground cinnamon

1/4 teaspoon ground cardamom

1 teaspoon lemon juice

1/2 cup sweet or dry red wine

1 head of romaine lettuce, washed for haroset sandwiches)

1. Blend all ingredients in food processor to form a paste. Roll into grape-sized balls.
   Put into a bowl, or on a pretty tray on top of lettuce, and leave near the head of table.
2. The leader rips off about a 3″ x 4″ piece of lettuce, flattens ball inside the leaf,
   folds leaf on itself to make a small haroset sandwich, and passes one to each guest.
3. Chill if not used immediately, and remove about 1 hour before Seder.

Yield: Serves 20-25.

MAKING MATZOH

The following morning, Mama and Papa put all the food
they had gathered during spring cleaning into a large box.
"Come, *shayna cups,*" Grandpa said, kissing each child
on the head, "tomorrow night is the first Passover Seder.
Let's take this box of *chametz* to the synagogue."
When they got there, he placed the food from their box into a much
bigger box. Other people had put their chametz into this box, too.
"Who's that can of bean-and-noodle soup for?" Harry asked.
"The temple gives all this food to people who are needy."
Grandpa patted Harry's belly and pulled him closer.
As more children arrived, Rabbi Ramsky came out of his office
and asked, "Would you all like to make matzoh today?"
Everyone nodded. He took them to a matzoh factory. In the kitchen,
a loud timer ticked away on the table as they mixed the ingredients.
The rabbi gave each child a ball of dough and shouted, "Hurry!"
They pounded, kneaded, and rolled out the mixture into flat, round circles.
Harry flicked some flour on Sophie's nose. She flicked some back.
The rabbi drooped the dough over long wooden sticks to dry.
Then they used forks to poke tiny holes into the smooth dough.
Grandpa helped the rabbi put the Passover matzoh into the oven.
Minutes later, there was a loud buzz. Everyone held their ears.
"Done!" Grandpa cried aloud. "Start to finish in eighteen minutes!"
Rabbi Ramsky took the handmade matzoh from the enormous oven.
As the matzoh cooled, the rabbi said, "The Israelites left Egypt in
such a hurry, they didn't have time to knead the dough or let it rise.
As they traveled in the hot desert sun, the dough baked. Matzoh is
the bread that our ancestors ate during their Exodus."

"We eat it to remember," Grandpa said, sighing, "when we were slaves in Egypt."

"It's a *mitzvah* to eat matzoh," said Rabbi Ramsky. "A good deed."

Pearl dusted off her apron, happy to have made her own special matzoh.

When they got home, Papa helped Pearl and Sophie sew a matzoh

cover while Harry teased Avi with a piece of jellied gefilte fish.

"The Gefilte Golem!" he squealed, chasing Avi around the kitchen table.

"Always the little joker." Grandma smiled, pinching Harry's cheek.

When Mama saw the matzoh cover, she whispered in Pearl and Sophie's ears,

"I will always use and treasure this." Pearl's chest swelled with pride.

HOW TO MAKE MATZOH

Passover, also called the Feast of Unleavened Bread, lasts for eight days during which Jews do not eat Chametz. Chametz is leavened food made with yeast or the five species: wheat, barley, rye, spelt, and oats. The Ashkenazi Jews also avoid eating rice, corn, millet, and legumes. The Hebrew word chametz means "fermented dough." The ritual search for chametz takes place the night before Passover (erev Pesach). The search is done with a candle, feather, and wooden spoon in the corners of the kitchen and throughout the house, looking for crumbs. The following morning, before the Passover Seder (within five hours of sunrise), the chametz found in the search is burned. Shemura matzoh ("guarded matzoh") is made from grain that has been watched from the moment it is cut until it is baked. Making this matzoh occurs within eighteen minutes, preventing fermentation (rising) through contact with water. Religious Jews bake matzoh by hand on the day before Passover. This is the recipe that the cousins used to make their special Passover matzot mitzvah.

    2 pounds of kosher for Passover flour or Passover cake meal
    1 1/2-2 cups of spring water (bottled kosher)

1. Preheat oven (made clean and kosher for Passover!) to 450 degrees Farenheit.
2. Combine flour and water in a large mixing bowl. Knead dough by hand. Tear into eight balls. Flatten into 10-inch circles with rolling pin to around 1/8-inch thick.
3. Allow dough to air-dry a few minutes (by laying it over a long wooden pole so the sides of the dough droop evenly). Then put on a flour-dusted surface. Prick with a fork, making long rows (about 1/2 of an inch apart) of tiny holes in the dough.
4. Put on parchment-lined cookie sheet. Bake (around 7-10 minutes) until the flat round circles of matzoh are crisp and lightly browned.
    Yield: 8 matzot (plural of matzoh). Cool and store.
    Note: For a fun dessert, melt kosher chocolate in a double-boiler pot, then dip the matzoh, coating it with the chocolate. Allow to cool on waxed paper in the refrigerator.

HOW TO MAKE THE MATZOH COVER

Every year, Grandpa is the leader of the Seder. He places three stacked matzohs in the center of the table and covers them with a special cloth. They represent both the unity of the Jewish people as well as the three major divisions: Cohen, Levi, and Israelites. (This year, he is using the matzoh cover that Pearl and Sophie made together.) During the Seder, he breaks the middle matzoh, the *afikomen* (a Greek word meaning "dessert"), wraps the half in a cloth napkin, and hides it when the children are not looking. The search for the afikomen takes place later on in the Seder. (Waiting for the search is the hardest part!) Tradition has it that the one who finds the afikomen wins a treat.

Matzoh covers can be made out of cotton cloth, muslin, felt, or linen and decorated in many different ways (pens, yarn, embroidery thread, sequins, etc.). This is the way Pearl and Sophie made theirs, which everyone agreed would be used this year, and for years to come.

Scissors  Indelible (permanent) marker/pen
Blue/white cotton cloth Decorations: yarn, embroidery thread,
Thread and needles for sewing sequins, beads, gold/silver thread

1. Cut two pieces of cotton cloth into 12-inch squares, one white, one blue.
2. Stitch by hand (Pearl asked Papa to help, using the sewing machine), along the edge of three sides, leaving one side open to slip the three matzohs inside the pouch.
3. On the white side, draw the symbols of the Seder plate with indelible (permanent and washable) ink or Magic Markers. (Pearl and Sophie needed help to embroider and write the Hebrew letters.) Put the child's name and year on the back cover (blue side) of the fabric.

THE BLESSINGS

Two blessings are said when the matzoh is eaten at the Passover Seder.

This is the *motzi,* a prayer said before eating bread:
Baruch atah Adonai, Eloheinu melech ha-olam, hamotzi lechem min ha-aretz.

בָּרוּךְ אַתָּה יהוה אֱלֹהֵינוּ מֶלֶךְ הָעוֹלָם הַמּוֹצִיא לֶחֶם מִן הָאָרֶץ.

This is the special prayer recited over the matzoh before it is eaten:
Baruch atah Adonai, Eloheinu melech ha-olam, asher kid-shanu b'mitzvotov v'tzivanu al achilat matzoh.

בָּרוּךְ אַתָּה יהוה אֱלֹהֵינוּ מֶלֶךְ הָעוֹלָם אֲשֶׁר קִדְשָׁנוּ בְּמִצְוֹתָיו וְצִוָּנוּ
עַל אֲכִילַת מַצָּה.

THE MYSTERY OF THE MISSING BREAD CRUMBS

Papa hid a few bread crumbs for the children to find later that evening
in the ritual search for any bits of bread that might be left in the house.
What he didn't know was that Cousin Harry had been watching him!
Harry hid in his pocket every crumb Papa had planted for the search.
When everyone gathered together to hunt for the chametz,
Harry swirled his camp flashlight. "A professional," Grandma teased.
The cousins followed Papa around the four corners of the kitchen as he held
a candle and poked in the pantry. Pearl dusted with a fluffy feather the drawers
and cabinets for any leftover crumbs as her brother held a wooden spoon.
"The cupboards are empty!" shouted Sophie with disappointment.
Papa seemed confused and wondered, *Where could the bread crumbs be?*
When no one was looking, Harry took the bits of bread he had hid in his
pocket earlier in the day, and placed them way on the back of a shelf.
After everyone searched everywhere, Harry squealed,
"I found bread crumbs!" And he put them in Papa's tiny chametz box.

16

"Sure you did," Sophie muttered under her breath, peeking in the box.

Papa was puzzled that the crumbs had suddenly appeared again.

"Hmm, I wonder where those came from?" he asked, scratching his head.

"You can't pull the wool over our eyes," Sophie said to Harry.

"Time to go to sleep now," Papa said. "Tomorrow night is Passover!"

"You know why tomorrow night is different from all other nights?"
Harry asked. "Because tomorrow we get to stay up late!"

"Go to bed, Harry." Papa sighed, carrying him on his shoulders
and chuckling to himself about his nephew's little joke.

The children were so excited, they had trouble falling asleep.

Grandma and Grandpa heard the children talking and giggling, so they
tiptoed downstairs. Grandma said, "Come, *kinder-le*." The children gathered
under a big quilt, their toes touching, as Grandma and Grandpa began to tell
the Passover story.

THE STORY OF PASSOVER

"Passover," said Grandpa, "is a Festival of Freedom. The *Haggadah*, the book we will read at our Seders, means 'narration' or 'telling.'"

The cousins huddled closer as Grandma started in a soft voice. "Thousands of years ago, the Jewish people were slaves in Egypt. How they were freed is the story we will pass on to you." Even Grandpa leaned closer. "Do you remember Joseph and the Coat of Many Colors?" Little heads nodded. "Well, he became the governor of the land of Egypt. When there was no food in the land of Canaan, his father, Jacob, and all of Joseph's brothers and their families settled in Egypt. The Egyptians accepted them even though they were different. Over many years, the Israelites grew in number. A new Pharaoh came to rule Egypt. He feared the Israelites would side with his enemies in a war. So he made them his slaves. The children of Israel built pyramids in the desert under the hot sun. They had hard, bitter lives working with brick and mortar, but still, the number of Israelites continued to grow. So the Pharaoh ordered that all male Israelites be killed at birth."

Avi and Harry gasped. A sudden hush fell on the room.

"Hey, this is the story of Moses," Sophie said smugly.

"Yes," said Grandpa as Grandma took a sip of tea. "After Moses was born, his mother, Yocheved, hid him for three months. She was afraid he would be found, so she built a basket of reeds and placed him in it on the banks of the river Nile. Miriam, Moses' older sister, waited, hidden in the bulrush, to see what would happen to her baby brother. When the Pharaoh's daughter, Bithya, came down to the river to bathe, she discovered the basket. She saw the baby inside and, guided by Miriam, ordered Moses' mother to be his nurse. Moses' mother did not tell anyone she was the baby's real mother. He was adopted by the Pharaoh's daughter and became a prince of Egypt.

One day, when Moses was a young man, he saw an Egyptian beating a Jewish slave. He became so angry at this injustice, he killed the Egyptian. Fearing for his life, he ran away. During that time, God visited Moses in the wilderness of Sinai, where he was tending his sheep, and spoke to him from the flames of a burning bush. 'Go back to Egypt, free your people and bring them out of the land of affliction into the land of milk and honey. Go tell Pharaoh, "Let My people go!"'"

Harry's eyes widened with excitement. "A burning bush!"

"Well," Grandma continued, "Moses said, 'Who am I to tell Pharaoh what to do?' And God said, 'I will be by your side and show the children of Israel signs so they will believe you were sent by me.' And the Lord asked Moses, 'What is in your hand?' Moses answered, 'A rod.' God said, 'Throw it on the ground.' And the rod, a shepherd's staff, became a serpent. Then the Lord said to Moses, 'Put out your hand. Place it inside your robe next to your chest.' When he took his hand out, it was leprous, as white as snow. Then God ordered Moses to return his hand to his chest. It turned to ordinary flesh again. 'If the Israelites do not believe these two signs, said the Lord, 'then take the water of the river Nile, pour it upon dry land, and the river will become a sea of blood.'"

Grandma paused. "It says in the Bible that Moses was 'slow of speech and tongue.' God told him that his brother, Aaron, spoke well and would help him. So Moses went back to Egypt and, with his brother, Aaron, showed his people the signs. The children of Israel bowed their heads and worshiped. Moses and Aaron went to the Pharaoh and said, "The God of Israel says 'Let My people go!' And the Pharaoh replied, 'Who is this God who says, 'Let My people go'? I know of no such God.' Moses answered, 'There is only one God. You pray to idols.' Pharaoh cried out, 'I will not let Israel go!" He ordered that the Israelites would no longer receive straw to make bricks. They would have to gather their own "stubble." So the Jewish slaves were scattered throughout Egypt. They spent time looking for straw, while the slave masters forced them to make the same amount of bricks as before. The Israelites were angry with Moses and said, 'Now things are worse than before. You promised that God would help.'"

"Where *was* God?" Pearl interrupted. "You're supposed to keep promises."

"God did," Grandpa said.

"How?" asked Harry, fidgeting.

Grandma sighed, "Tomorrow night we will remember and celebrate our journey. Right now"—she yawned—"I am making an exodus to the bedroom so that I get some sleep. I would like all my sweet little lambs to do the same." She gave each one a kiss on the head. Grandpa tucked them in, and they were fast asleep before Grandma and Grandpa tiptoed upstairs.

PLACE MAT OF THE EXODUS FROM EGYPT

Following the journey of the Israelites will keep Pearl and her cousins busy during some of the long parts of the Seder reading. Every year at one point, Uncle Solly starts falling asleep. Last Passover, he yawned, "I'll pick you up at the Plagues."

Parchment paper or	White paste or rubber cement
cream-colored drawing paper	Crayons, colored pencils,
Brewed tea	watercolors, washable markers
Paintbrush	Clear glue
Bristol board/oak tag	Clear acetate

1. Use parchment paper from an art store—or, brew strong tea to make your own old-looking paper. (Grandma made extra to sip from another mug while the tea bag was seeping.) Crumple a piece of 11″ x 14″ cream-colored drawing paper. Smooth out surface to flatten. With a paintbrush, brush tea so it stains the creases in the paper. Let the paper dry. Ask an adult to slightly burn the edges of the piece of paper, to give it the feeling of an ancient map.
2. Paste the "parchment" onto an 11″ x 14″ piece of bristol board or oak tag, using white paste or rubber cement. Now you have your flat "place mat" surface to work on.
3. Draw your own map—or copy the journey on the facing page—onto the paper. (Same size or enlarge.) With crayons, colored pencils, watercolors, or washable markers, color in the special events, like the parting of the Red Sea, or wandering in the Sinai.
4. Dab clear glue in each corner of an 11″ x 14″ piece of clear acetate. (You can buy this at any art supply store.) Put it on top of place mat. (For the first two Seders, Pearl used only her finger to trace the journey, since she was not allowed to write—just as on Shabbat—but other times, she followed the path of the Exodus using washable markers on the clear acetate surface.)

Exodus from Egypt

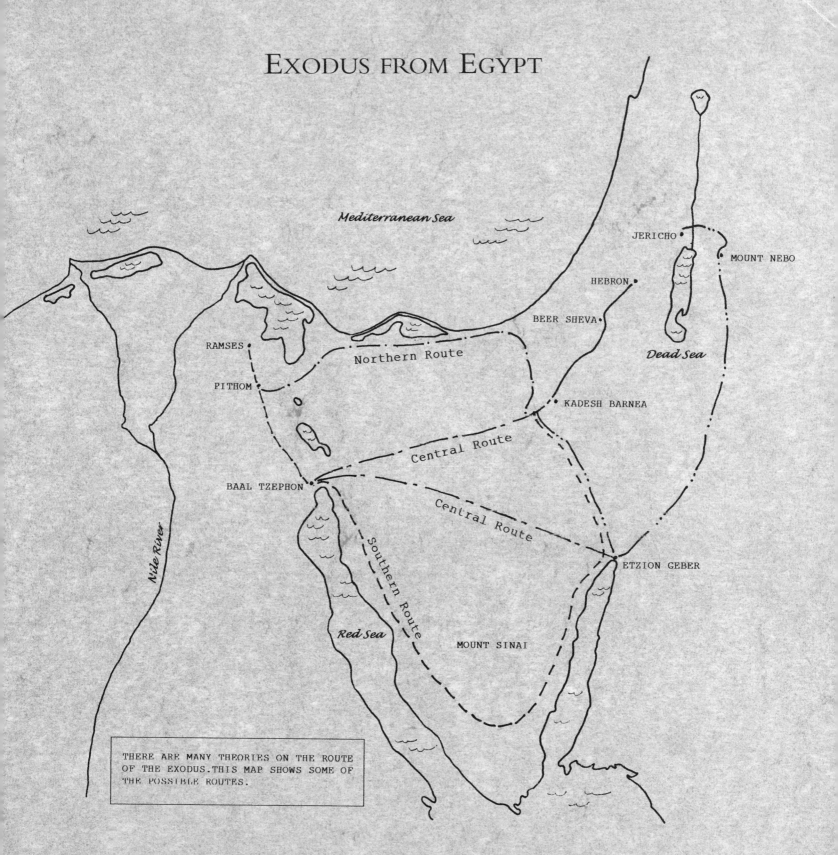

THERE ARE MANY THEORIES ON THE ROUTE
OF THE EXODUS. THIS MAP SHOWS SOME OF
THE POSSIBLE ROUTES.

Papa Burns the Chametz

At sunrise, Pearl awoke to the smell of something sharp in the air.
Papa was in the garden making a small fire on top of some rocks.
Pearl went outside to watch as she rubbed her eyes and yawned.
Papa smiled and put his arm around her. "Get Avi and your cousins."
One by one, they marched down the porch steps into the backyard.
Papa began to burn the bits of chametz. When the last crumb was gone,
and the flames went out, Papa said, "*Now* I am ready for Pesach!"
Mama was already cooking when they got inside the kitchen.
"Can I have some *matzoh brei* for breakfast?" Pearl asked. "I'll help."
Pearl dreamed all year of these matzoh pancakes smothered in maple syrup.
"Tomorrow," Mama said. And then she said to Papa as they cleared
the table, "We have a lot to do before the Seder tonight. How can
we keep the children busy?" Sophie, always the boss, said,
"I'll make a list of what *we* need to do."

SOPHIE'S LIST OF THINGS TO DO

Sophie wrote on a pad, "Number one: Make place cards for each guest."

"Good idea," said Harry. "We'll draw a plague in the corner of each card."

He wiggled a rubber bug in front of his sister Sophie's face.

"I'm real scared," Sophie said, not even looking up.

Avi whispered to Pearl, "I don't want to be a bug. Can I be a frog?"

"Avi," said Pearl, "it's the Plagues! One isn't better than the other!"

"Not a bug," he insisted. "They're noisy and annoying."

"Yeah, like Harry," Sophie added. Pearl and Avi laughed.

Avi raised his hand. "Y-e-es?" Sophie tapped her pencil.

"Can I make a Moses place card instead?" he asked.

"Sure, Moses, matzoh, whatever," Sophie continued. "Number two?"

"We made finger puppets in Sunday school," Avi said, smiling.

"And we made Elijah's cup," Pearl added.

"Put them down, Soph," Harry said, "even if they're not *your* ideas."

"We made Miriam's timbrel," Sophie said out loud as she scribbled.

"What's that?" Pearl smiled and moved her chair closer to Sophie's.

"Tambourines. What number am I at?" Sophie asked Pearl impatiently.

"Number two, puppets. Number three, cup. Number four? Drums . . ."

Pearl's voice trailed off as Sophie stared up in the air.

"How about we make pillows?" suggested Pearl. "To lean on.
Grandpa always uses mine from my bed. He got matzoh
crumbs and wine all over my new pillowcase last year."

"We have to help set the table, too." Sophie said.

"Write Seder Plate—" Harry glared at his sister— "In case you forget."

"Number seven," continued Sophie, "put Harry's place setting in the basement by the boiler. Under the spiderwebs." She began to giggle.

As they began to draw, Harry pestered Avi. "Tonight's the night. It's *your* turn. You're the youngest at the Seder. And you know what?"

"You *have* to ask the Four Questions," Sophie piped in.

Avi looked up, a little scared, but he said, "I'm ready."

"He'll be a whiz." Pearl had been practicing with Avi for weeks.

PASSOVER PLACE CARDS

Since Avi and Harry both wanted Moses on their place cards, Sophie suggested, "Let's pick from a hat." Pearl wrote each guest's name on a different slip of colored paper. She put them facedown in Grandpa's hat. She did the same for some of the symbols and Bible characters of Passover, some Plagues—like frogs, making them red, green, and purple—and placed them in Papa's baseball cap. Then each child took a turn. They picked them out of the hats, matching the colors.

Small index cards	Tiny clear beads
Gold/silver markers	Glitter (dark brown, copper)
White glue	Pipe cleaners
Cotton/kosher salt	Origami paper

1. Fold an index card in half with the lined side inward. (The blank white surface, on the outside, is to write, draw, or paint on.)

2. Write each guest's name with a gold or silver marker (found in a stationery or art supply store). Using crayons and markers, decorate the card with a bug, a frog, a matzoh, the Red Sea, or maybe Moses, Aaron, Miriam, etc., so that each place card has a different picture.

3. To represent "hail," glue tiny pieces of cotton, kosher salt, or tiny clear beads used in decorating sweaters (found in trimming or notions stores in the sewing department) onto the index card. For grains of dust, glue on dark-colored glitter.

4. Colored pipe cleaners can be used to make spiders, frogs, animals, etc.
   Optional: Fold animals and insects out of origami paper. Hang over the top corner of the card. Fasten using white glue.

HOW TO MAKE FINGER PUPPETS

The cousins made different kinds of puppets. On the night of the first Seder, they put one in front of each place setting next to a place card. On the second night, they gathered the puppets in a wicker strawberry basket and acted out the Passover story. "Oy," Grandma said, shaking her head, "to have such talent in one family, I'm kvelling. You're all geniuses," she said, proudly. You will need:

Scissors, pencils, cardboard, oak tag/manila paper, white glue, cotton, toothpicks, crayons, Magic Markers, muslin/burlap, nontoxic washable markers, turquoise beads, black origami paper, gold thread, black pipe cleaners, white crepe paper/white cloth

keyhole shape

5"

holes for fingers

1. Draw a 5″ tall cardboard form in the shape a keyhole (see diagram). Cut out shape. Cut two holes at bottom for a child's index and middle fingers, which become the "legs" of the finger puppets.

2. Trace keyhole shape and two circle holes again onto a manila folder or oak tag. Using a small amount of white glue, paste the manila paper on top of the cardboard form Press down with heavy book until dry.

3. Here are a few ideas for decorating the puppets:

    Moses: Paste cotton for hair and white beard. Trace triangle part of body onto striped cloth. Duplicate holes for two fingers. Glue onto manila paper. Then glue a small twig, or brown pipe cleaner for his shepherd's staff.

    sandals on fingers

    Miriam: Glue 3″ to 4″ strands of yarn for hair. Trace keyhole shape onto colorful fabric for a dress. Wrap yarn or 1/16″ thick plain ribbon around chest and tie on back. Use crayon or Magic Markers to color a bottom border around the finger holes.

    punch holes

    Israelites: Cut muslin or burlap cloth to fit body. Glue to manila paper. Leave bottom open (for fingers). Optional: Draw sandals with nontoxic washable markers on child's two fingers that once again will become the "legs."

    Egyptians: Glue tiny turquoise beads for a necklace. Fold black origami paper in small accordion fan for hair. Glue thin gold thread across forehead. Use black pipe cleaner for beards. (See diagram for shape to form.) Use white crepe paper for clothing.

THE FOUR CHILDREN PUPPETS

During the Seder, we tell a parable of four children who ask questions. This shows we all have many sides. Everybody has the capacity to be wise, wicked, innocent, and ignorant. Asking questions, discussing the answers with children, are important parts of the Seder.

The wise child asks, *What are the customs and laws of Passover?*

The wicked one asks, *What does this Seder mean to all of you?*

The innocent child asks, *What does this all mean?*

And then there is the child *who does not know how to ask.*

You will need: Tongue depressor, embroidery thread, Magic Markers, white glue, scissors, pipe cleaners

1. Draw different expressions on each stick with Magic Markers.
2. Glue embroidery thread "hair" to top of tongue depressor around the face.
3. Fasten pipe cleaners to the back of depressor with glue to make arms and legs (see diagram). Below are the puppets the cousins made: Pearl chose the wise one; Harry, the wicked one (big surprise); Avi ended up being the innocent one; and Sophie, the one who doesn't know how to ask.

RECLINING PILLOW

On all other nights, we sit up straight or recline; why on this night do we only recline? One answer is that we are no longer slaves in Egypt. Now we are free to relax.

You will need: Scissors, felt (various colors), muslin or cotton cloth (pale color), sequins, multicolored yarn, embroidery or cotton thread, Poly-Fil (or old stockings)

1. Cut two 12″ x 12″ pieces of muslin or cotton cloth.
2. Stitch with yarn, embroidery, or cotton thread along three sides of the cloth 1/2″ from edge.
3. Cut felt in shapes of stems, leaves, or flowers and glue down onto pillow surface.
4. Sew sequins around border of flower designs (see diagram).
5. Stuff with Poly-Fil (from a sewing supply or crafts store), or old nylon stockings.
6. Sew open side 1/2″ from edge to close pillow.

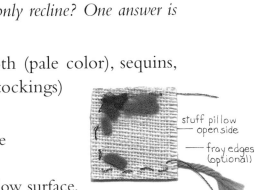

ELIJAH'S CUP

One lifts and drinks Four Cups of Wine during the Seder. In addition, a large goblet (A Fifth Cup of Wine) is filled and left in the center of the Seder table to honor the Prophet Elijah. According to the Bible, Elijah never died. He was lifted to the heavens in a chariot of fire. Many believe he will appear again with the coming of the Messiah. It is tradition to open the front door in the hope that he will visit, drink from this cup, and bring lasting peace on earth.

Scissors

Cardboard

Gold or silver spray paint

Colorful beads

Empty film canister (or empty spool of thread)

Clear glue

Plastic cup (clear tumbler, 5 ounce)

Gold-braided trim (around 1/4″ height)

Small gold- or silver-colored dessert plate

1. Cut a circle 3 1/2″ in diameter out of heavy cardboard; spray-paint gold or silver. Glue and decorate the edge of the circle with jewel-like beads (found in craft store).
2. Spray-paint a film canister with cap still attached in gold or silver. Allow to dry. Glue bottom of canister to the cardboard circle, creating the stem and base for the goblet.
3. Using clear glue, attach plastic tumbler to top of canister. Glue band of gold-braided trim (found in sewing stores) 1/2 inch from rim (optional).
4. You now have Elijah's Cup. Fill it with sweet red wine or grape juice. Place on a small silver- or gold-colored dessert plate. Wait for Elijah.

Many Seder tables now include Miriam's Cup, which you can make and fill with spring water instead of wine. According to *midrash*, when Miriam, Moses' sister, died, the well of water that accompanied the Israelites throughout the desert during their Exodus from Egypt ran dry. You can recite, "This is the cup of Miriam, the cup of living waters."

MIRIAM'S TIMBRELS

After Pharaoh let the children of Israel leave Egypt, he changed his mind and sent his army to bring them back. As the Israelites passed safely through the Red Sea, the water suddenly parted, creating walls on either side of them. The entire Egyptian army running after them was drowned. Miriam, Moses and Aaron's sister, led the women out of the parted sea "dancing with timbrels (tambourines)." During the forty years of wandering in the desert, the Israelites were blessed with fresh water, referred to as "Miriam's well." It is a recent custom to honor this brave woman, who helped the Jewish people survive the Exodus to the Promised Land.

Small Drum	*Tambourines*
Pencil or Magic Marker	Two Styrofoam dinner plates
Empty coffee can with plastic lid	Stapler or white glue
Scissors	Hole puncher or scissors
Stretchable fabric (like Spandex)	Thin silk ribbons, for streamers
Large, thick rubber band	(about 3/16″ to 1/4″ thick)
White glue	Ruler or tape measure
Decorative ribbon (about 1/2″)	Small jingle bells (available at
	crafts store)

1. *For a small drum:* Using a pencil, trace the coffee can lid onto the fabric. Measure 3/4″ past the edge of the circle—and cut on the line.
2. Stretch cloth tightly across one end of can—the top—and place plastic lid on the other end—the bottom. Fasten in place with a sturdy rubber band.
3. Glue decorative or embroidered ribbon on rubber band. Allow to dry.

1. *For a tambourine:* Staple or glue two plates together. Allow to dry.
2. Punch holes in four "corners" of plates.
3. Loop three 20″ long strands of ribbons (for streamers) halfway through holes, and knot together (see diagram).
4. Knot each strand of ribbon through a slit in bell and tie near hole of plate.

knot ribbon through
slit in bell
pie plates

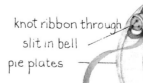

THE SEDER PLATE

1. Egg *(beitzah)*: The roasted egg recalls the time when sacrificial offerings were made in the Temple in Jerusalem. The egg is also a symbol of fertility and new life.

2. Shank bone *(zeroa)*: A burnt portion of a bone representing the paschal offering in memory of the ancient Temple sacrifice. (For vegetarians, an alternative is a broiled beet.)

3. Bitter herbs *(maror)*: Usually horseradish, sometimes romaine lettuce. Signifies the bitterness of slavery.

4. *Ḥaroset*: Sweet paste of chopped apples, nuts, and cinnamon, mixed with a sweet red wine. The fruit-and-nut mixture symbolizes the mortar and bricks the Israelites used to build pyramids when they were in bondage to the Pharaohs in Egypt. The red wine is a reminder that God parted the Red Sea during the Exodus.

5. Parsley *(karpas)*: A parsley sprig stands for spring, life, and hope. Parsley dipped in salt water suggests the salty tears of the slaves.

6. Grated horseradish *(ḥazeret)*: Additional bitter herb eaten with the *ḥaroset* in the *matzoh* sandwich *(korekh)*. Shows that life has two sides—bitter and sweet.

30

HOW TO MAKE A SEDER PLATE

Avi and Harry made their own designs with crayons and Magic Markers on plain white paper plates. (Styrofoam and plastic-coated ones are also fine.) Here are other ideas:

Colored tissue paper

Magic Markers

Scissors

Shellac (optional)

Regular gray clay or Fimo

Poster paints

Silver paper muffin cups

Food for symbols on Seder Plate

Dessert or dinner plates, paper or plastic

Craft kits (bought in crafts store)

1. Plate idea number one: Draw symbols of food on colored tissue paper with Magic Markers. Cut out with scissors. Paste onto plastic-coated or paper dessert plate. (To give it a stained-glass look, Pearl's papa brushed the plate with shellac, then let it dry.)

2. Plate idea number two: Use regular or Fimo clay (can be found in an art supply or crafts store) to sculpt symbols. Allow to dry. (Apply poster paint if regular clay. Fimo comes in many different colors.) Display on white dinner plate on Seder table.

3. Plate idea number three: Draw symbols on white paper plate. Place a silver paper muffin cup (from baking section of supermarket) on top of each symbol. Put real food in each cup before the Seder and use new cups on the second night.

Note: *Matzoh,* is a reminder that the Hebrews left Egypt in such haste the bread didn't have time to rise. Three *matzot* on a separate plate are covered with a special cloth and placed to the right of the Seder Plate. These *matzot* represent the three tribes of Israel. The *afikomen* (a Greek word meaning "dessert") is the middle *matzoh,* which is hidden during the Seder. Children search for it at the end of the meal, and the one who finds it wins a treat!

OUT OF EGYPT

After breakfast, the children cut, pasted, painted, and sewed.
Grandma and Grandpa sat on the floor and helped them.
Avi tugged at Grandpa's sleeve, and smiled up at him.
"You never finished the story of Passover. Could we hear it?"
Harry took the rubber bug from his pajama pocket and tossed it in the air.
It landed in Avi's lap. He squirmed and yelled, "Leaping locusts!"
"Exactly," said Grandpa. "God visited Ten Plagues on the Egyptians
because Pharaoh would not let the Israelites leave Egypt. So God showed
Pharaoh that there was only one true God by punishing the Egyptians
with Ten Plagues. It was after suffering the Tenth Plague that Pharaoh
freed the children of Israel from Egypt. Here is what happened to Pharaoh
and the Egyptians."
Grandpa drew a chart onto a large piece of oak tag.

1. *Dahm:* Blood

דָּם

For one week, God turned the waters of the Nile—the source of food and drink—into a river of blood. The fish died; the river became foul. Only the land of Goshen, where the Israelites lived, had water.

2. *Tzfardeh-ah:* Frogs

צְפַרְדֵּעַ

Pharaoh still would not let Moses' people go. So God said, "Tell your brother Aaron, 'Stretch your hand with a rod over the rivers, canals and pools, and cause frogs to rise over Egypt.'" Frogs were in the rivers, houses, beds, ovens, kneading bowls, everywhere, covering the land of Egypt. Pharaoh still refused.

3. *Ki-nim:* Lice

כִּנִּים

So Aaron stretched his rod into the earth's dust. Lice bit man and beast. The Pharaoh's own magicians could not help. They said, "This must be a sign of God's presence." The Lord told Moses, "Rise up in the morning, go to Pharaoh, tell him to let My people go." Pharaoh wouldn't listen.

4. *Arov:* Bugs

עָרוֹב

The "scarab," or beetle, was the sacred emblem of the Egyptian Sun-god. It was sculptured on monuments and tombs, engraved on gems and amulets, and honored in all Egyptian images. God said, "Goshen will be set apart from the rest of Egypt. You will stand on the border, look toward Egypt, and see swarms of bugs. In Goshen, there will be none." Pharaoh continued to ignore God's request to let the Israelites go.

5. *Dever:* Cattle disease

דֶּבֶר

Then the Egyptians' cattle, horses, donkeys, and camels died while herds and flocks of the families of Israel lived. The Pharaoh continued to say no, and the Israelites remained in slavery.

6. *Sh'hin:* Boils

שְׁחִין

Moses threw soot toward the heavens in the sight of Pharaoh. It became a fine dust and caused boils on people and animals. Even Pharaoh's magicians were unable to imitate what he did. Again, the Jews were spared.

7. *Barad:* Hail

בָּרָד

The Lord then told Moses to hold his rod toward the sky. Thunder roared, and hail fell across "every herb of the field." Lightning caused fire, killing everything in its path.

8. *Ar-beh:* Locusts

אַרְבֶּה

When the rain, hail, and thunder ended, the Pharaoh still remained unmoved. The land of Goshen continued to be spared while locusts were brought to the borders of Egypt. Whatever crops were left after the hailstorm were eaten by locusts. Egypt became a wasteland. Pharaoh's servants pleaded with him to let the Israelites go. But he didn't.

9. *Ḥoshekh:* Darkness

חֹשֶׁךְ

A thick, heavy cloud hung over the land and hid the sun. No one moved for three days. But the children of Israel had light in their homes. Finally, the Pharaoh said, "Leave, but your flocks and herds have to stay." He realized they would have to come back for their animals. Moses said, "I will not return to Egypt." So Pharaoh took back his offer.

10. *Makat B'horot:* Death of the firstborn

מַכַּת בְּכוֹרוֹת

God told Moses, "There will be one last plague and a cry in the land of Egypt unlike any that has come." Moses told the people, "At dusk, mark your doorposts. That night, eat unleavened bread and bitter herbs. If anything is left in the morning, burn it with fire. Then, wearing sandals, and with a staff in hand, eat in haste. (This was the first Passover Seder.) God will go through the land of Egypt and kill the firstborn of man and beast. The marked homes will be passed over by the Angel of Death. You will eat unleavened bread for seven days and observe this feast for generations to come."

THE GUESTS ARRIVE

Pearl and her cousins helped set the table with the things
they had made. Then Pearl put pansies she had picked into
a vase and placed it in the center as everyone got ready.
She sat on the front porch in her new dress and sweater
waiting for friends to arrive. She felt very special inside.
This was Pearl's favorite time of year: Spring.
And Passover was Pearl's favorite holiday.
By the time the sun sank in the sky, the guests had arrived.
After all the kissing and hugging, they sat down to begin.
Avi switched place cards with Harry so he could sit next to Pearl.
"In case I need help during the Four Questions," he whispered to her.
All the children sat at a card table at the end of the dining-room table.
"I'm going to wobble our table during the Plagues," Harry threatened.
"So wobble." Sophie shrugged as she neatened up her place setting.
"Shh," said Aunt Rachel as Grandpa sat down at the head of the table.

THE FIFTEEN STEPS OF THE SEDER

1.   קַדֵּשׁ   *Kadesh:* The First Kiddush over the Ritual Wine

2.   וּרְחַץ   *Urḥatz:* Washing Hands

3.   כַּרְפַּס   *Karpas:* Fresh Greens Dipped in Salt Water

4.   יַחַץ   *Yaḥatz:* Breaking the Middle Matzoh in Half (Afikomen)

5.   מַגִּיד   *Maggid:* Telling the Story (there are four verses in the Torah)

6.   רָחְצָה   *Roḥtzah:* Washing Hands before Eating

7.   מוֹצִיא   *Motzi:* The Brakhah (Blessing) over the Bread

8.   מַצָּה   *Matzoh:* Blessing the Unleavened Bread

9.   מָרוֹר   *Maror:* Eating the Bitter Herb

10.   כּוֹרֵךְ   *Korekh:* The Hillel Sandwich (Bitter Herb/Ḥaroset on Matzoh)

11.   שֻׁלְחָן עוֹרֵךְ   *Shulḥan Orekh:* Serving the Meal (Means "the set table" in Hebrew)

12.   צָפוּן   *Tzafun:* Eating the Hidden Afikomen (Dessert)

13.   בָּרֵךְ   *Barekh:* Prayer After the Meal

14.   הַלֵּל   *Hallel:* Songs ("Halleluyah" comes from the Hebrew *hallel*)

15.   נִרְצָה   *Nirtzah:* A Final Wish for Peace and "Next Year in Jerusalem!"

THE PASSOVER SEDER

Grandma blessed and lit the candles.

Grandpa raised a silver Kiddush cup and said a blessing over the wine.

Since he was the leader of the Seder, he was the first to read. He recited

from the Haggadah that *his* father had brought over when he came to America.

Grandpa passed around a big copper pitcher filled with cold water.

Everyone took turns pouring some water over their hands into a bowl.

When it was Harry's turn, he splashed the bottom and got Sophie's

party dress wet. As she dried herself off with a dish towel,

she protested: "In case you didn't know, I already had a shower."

Then Grandpa ripped pieces of parsley off a sprig,

dipped them in salt water, and passed them to each guest.

Harry sighed. "When are we going to eat?"

He could hear Sophie's stomach grumbling, too.

Grandpa continued and said, "The salt reminds me of tears."

Pearl looked at her father. "It tastes like when we swim in the ocean."

Papa nodded. "Like the Red Sea that the Jews crossed to freedom."

All eyes were on Grandpa, especially Harry's, as Grandpa broke the *afikomen,*

the middle matzoh, in half, and put it in a white cloth napkin and left to hide it.

"Did you see where he hid it?" Harry asked.

He crawled between his aunts' and uncles' legs, searching.

"Have patience," Uncle Solly said. "You'll all look for it later."

Harry poked Avi from under the table. "You know what's next?"

"The Four Questions?" said Avi, poking him back.

Avi recited each question by heart, with a little help from Pearl,

Sophie, and Harry. "You did it!" They patted him on the back.

Avi smiled gleefully. Then everyone sang, "Mah Nishtanah."

"Where are my Four Children?" Grandpa asked.

They each waved their puppets high in the air.

Pearl held up the wise one. Harry, the wicked one.

Avi, the innocent. Sophie held the one who doesn't know how to ask.

Sophie said, "Tomorrow night, Pearl, I am going to be the wise one."

Harry added, "And I'm *not* being the wicked one. No way."

"To me," Grandma said with a big grin, "all my four grandchildren

are as sweet as the Four Cups of Wine we drink during the Seder."

All the parents groaned. "Someday, you'll be grandparents,"

Grandma said to everyone, "and you'll know exactly how I feel."

At the retelling of the Ten Plagues, everyone dipped their pinkies ten times

into their glasses of wine—the children had grape juice—

and said together the name of a Plague each time.

Harry licked his pinkie finger during the dip for lice. "*Oy!*" Grandma cried.

"Dab your grape juice on the plate not in your mouth!"

A tiny spider crept by. Sophie jumped and then realized it was

plastic, being pulled by a string. Harry was playing jokes again.

"*Dayenu,* Harry," said Uncle Solly. "Enough."

And then they all sang "Dayenu." Grandpa passed around pieces

of matzoh with bitter herbs and sweet haroset.

Harry took seconds on the haroset before eating the bitter herbs.

"I need chicken soup!" he moaned. "I'm starving!"

"It's coming. Soon." Mama got up to stir the matzoh ball soup.

When the hard-boiled eggs were brought out, Avi asked,

"What are the eggs doing in the salt water?"

"The back float!" Harry shouted out. Everyone laughed.

"Actually," Grandpa said, "eggs dipped in salt water

symbolize the mourning of the destruction of the Temple."

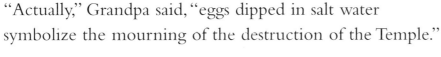

Grandma added, "But darling, also life and birth."

Then everyone, except the children, who held their noses, ate gefilte fish.

Finally it was the moment Harry was waiting for—the meal.

"Real food," sighed Harry as stuffed cabbage, brisket, *tsimmes,*

and two kinds of *kugel,* kept coming.

They were all so stuffed afterward, they could hardly move.

"Anyone need a little exercise?" Grandpa raised his eyebrows.

Harry shouted, "It's time to find the *afikomen!*"

The children ran around the house searching for the hidden matzoh.

"I found it!" Pearl screamed from under the couch in the living room.

Harry mumbled, "It's not fair." Grandpa gave a coin to each child,

not just Pearl. Grandma gave them each a big kiss and a big hug.

"Can Grandpa do magic? I didn't see him hide it," Avi said.

"Maybe he's—" Harry's voice deepened— "ELIJAH!"

Harry opened the front door for Elijah and screamed.

A neighbor was in the doorway, with a scarf over her head,

holding a plate filled with macaroons and orange sponge cake.

Mama placed the desserts next to Elijah's cup. Avi whispered,

"Pearl, I think some wine is missing. I think he came."

Pearl looked inside the cup. "Do you think so?" she asked.

"Did Grandpa sip any," Harry asked, "when no one was looking?"

Harry looked at Papa, and Papa winked at him, both remembering

how Harry had hid the bread crumbs when no one was looking.

"Grandpa wouldn't do that," Pearl insisted.

"But Harry will when he's a grandfather," Sophie teased.

Harry grinned as they said blessings and sang songs.

Friends and family put their arms around each other,

forming a chain as they swayed back and forth to sing "Chad Gadya."

At the end of the Seder, everyone cried, "Next year in Jerusalem!"

Aunt Rachel and Uncle Solly shouted, "Next year in New Jersey!"

Grandma and Grandpa added, "Next year at our condo in Florida!"
Everyone cried, "Too hot and muggy!"
Mama and Papa said together, "Next year here again."
Pearl said softly to her brother, "I know something we should add to the Seder—the Eleventh Plague: The Return of Sophie and Harry."
"I heard that," they said at the same time.
"Just kidding," Pearl and Avi answered.
Pearl put her pink bracelet on Sophie. "It matches your shoes."
And Sophie gave her a purple ribbon. "For tomorrow night."
Everyone went outside under the starry sky.
The air was cool and crisp, and smelled sweet.
"I can hardly wait until tomorrow night," Harry said.
"Tomorrow night will definitely be a different night."
"Why?" Everybody asked Harry together.
"I feel lucky about finding that afikomen!" he said.
Everyone laughed, Uncle Solly hugged Harry.
Pearl, Avi, and Sophie agreed to let him have his chance.
And they decided to keep it a secret just between them.

THE FOUR QUESTIONS

The youngest child present asks:

Why is this night different from all other nights?

מַה נִּשְׁתַּנָּה הַלַּיְלָה הַזֶּה מִכָּל הַלֵּילוֹת.

On all other nights we eat bread or matzoh:
Why tonight only matzoh?

שֶׁבְּכָל הַלֵּילוֹת אָנוּ אוֹכְלִין חָמֵץ וּמַצָּה
הַלַּיְלָה הַזֶּה כֻּלוֹ מַצָּה.

On all other nights we eat any kind of herb:
Why tonight only bitter herb?

שֶׁבְּכָל הַלֵּילוֹת אָנוּ אוֹכְלִין שְׁאָר יְרָקוֹת
הַלַּיְלָה הַזֶּה מָרוֹר.

On all other nights we don't dip the herbs even once:
Why tonight do we dip twice?

שֶׁבְּכָל הַלֵּילוֹת אֵין אָנוּ מַטְבִּילִין אֲפִלּוּ פַּעַם אֶחָת
הַלַּיְלָה הַזֶּה שְׁתֵּי פְעָמִים.

On all other nights we eat either sitting or reclining:
Why tonight do we all recline?

שֶׁבְּכָל הַלֵּילוֹת אָנוּ אוֹכְלִין בֵּין יוֹשְׁבִין וּבֵין מְסֻבִּין
הַלַּיְלָה הַזֶּה כֻּלָנוּ מְסֻבִּין.

Mah Nishtanah
"Why is this Night?"

DAYENU (It Would Have Been Enough For Us)

This ancient hymn thanks God for the miracles of the Exodus. Grandpa was the leader and read each line. Everybody chanted "Dayenu" together at the end of each phrase.

If God had taken us out of Egypt without punishing the Egyptians
It would have been enough for us. *Dayenu.* (Repeat after every line.)
If God had punished the Egyptians and not cast judgment on their gods . . .
If God had cast judgment on their gods and not slain their firstborn . . .
If God had slain their firstborn and not given us their riches . . .
If God had given us their riches and not divided the sea for us . . .
If God had divided the sea for us and not led us to dry land . . .
If God led us to dry land and not drowned the Egyptians chasing us . . .
If God had drowned the Egyptians chasing us and not taken care of us in the
     desert forty years . . .
If God had taken care of us in the desert forty years without feeding us manna . . .
If God had fed us manna without giving us the Sabbath . . .
If God had given us the Sabbath without bringing us to Mount Sinai . . .
If God had brought us to Mount Sinai without giving us the Torah . . .
If God had given us the Torah and not brought us into the land of Israel . . .
If God had brought us into the land of Israel without building us the Temple . . .
It would have been enough for us. *Dayenu.*
But God did all these great deeds.

Dayenu

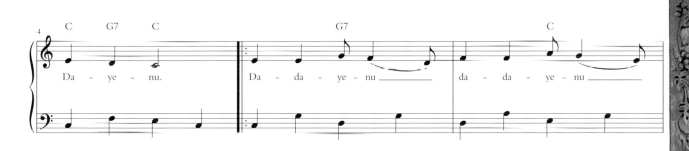

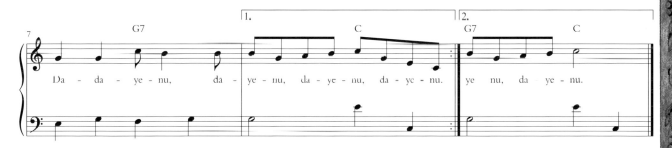

Chad Gadya (One Little Goat)

One little goat, one little goat,
That my father bought for two *zuzim*.
(One little goat.) Chad Gadya.

Then came the cat that ate the goat
That my father bought for two *zuzim*.
Chad Gadya.

Then came the dog that bit the cat
That ate the goat . . . *(continue verse)*
Then came the stick that beat the dog
That bit the cat
That ate the goat . . . *(etc.)*

Then came the fire that burned the stick
That beat the dog
That bit the cat . . . *(and continue verses)*

Then came the water that put out the fire
That burned the stick . . .

Then came the ox that drank the water
That put out the fire . . .

Then came the butcher who slew the ox
That drank the water . . .

Then came the Angel of Death who killed the butcher
Who slew the ox . . .

Then came the Holy One, Blessed be God
Who killed the Angel of Death
Who killed the butcher
Who slew the ox
That drank the water
That put out the fire
That burned the stick
That beat the dog
That bit the cat
That ate the goat
That my father bought for two zuzim.
Chad Gadya!

Chad Gadya

This song is fun at the end of the Passover Seder, but it is also thought to be an allegory. Israel is "the kid" or little goat bought by God for two zuzim (the two tablets of the Ten Commandments, or Moses and Aaron, who led the Exodus from Egypt.) All the animals in the song symbolize the appearance of Israel's enemies, and then their disappearance. The Pharaoh had a dream of a scale. On one side of the balance were the people of Mitzrayim. On the other lay a "young kid." He feared from this dream that a child of Israel would be born who would lead his people to freedom. The ending of "Chad Gadya" is one of joy and overcoming oppressors.

GLOSSARY

Afikomen (A-fee-CO-men): a Greek word for "dessert," the middle matzoh hidden during the seder

Chametz (HA-mets): any food that is made from a grain that has risen or fermented

Dayenu (DYE-ey-new): "It would have been enough for us"

Gefilte fish (Ga-FILL-ta fish): boned and simmered balls of whitefish, carp, or pike

Golem (GO-lem): in Hebrew, means "matter without shape" (Psalm 139:16); in Jewish folklore, a clumsy figure sculpted (often from clay) into human form that came to life

Haggadah (ha-GOD-da): Hebrew for "telling"; a narrative read aloud at the Seder table from the book of Exodus in the Talmud during the Passover holiday by Jews throughout the world

Ḥaroset (HA-row-set): a paste made of chopped fruit (apples and dates) and nuts with red wine

Kiddush (Kid-dooch): a blessing

Kinder-le (KIN-der-la): an affectionate Yiddish term for "children" from the German word, *kinder*

Kugel (KU-gull): potato or noodle pudding

Latke (LOT-ka): a potato pancake fried in oil

Mandelbrot (MON-dell-bread): an almond loaf sliced into oblong cookies and toasted

Matzoh (MOTT-sa): unleavened (no yeast) flat bread eaten during Passover holiday

Matzoh brei (MOTT-sa brei—as in "eye"): a matzoh-and-egg pancake fried in butter

Midrash (MID-rash): Hebrew Bible story and interpretation by a scholar from the Torah

Mitzvah (MITS-va): a good deed and kind act

Oy! (Oy!): Yiddish for an exclamation or cry of astonishment and amazement

Pesach (PAY-sokh, with a gutteral "kh"): Passover holiday in Hebrew; to "pass over"

Pharaoh (FAIR-row): an ancient Egyptian king

Rabbi (RA-bye): an ordained religious leader of a Jewish congregation

Schmoozing (SHMOOZ-ing): friendly talk, chitchat, or a bit of harmlesss gossip

Seder (SAY-der): In Hebrew, means "order" the name of a ritual meal telling the Passover story

Shayna cup (SHAY-na cup): Yiddish for "beautiful head"; a term of endearment

Tsimmes (SIM-ess): stewed sweet potatoes, carrots, and prunes